TREK OR TREAT

Terry Flanagan and Eleanor Ehrhardt

BALLANTINE BOOKS • NEW YORK

INTRODUCTION

STAR TREK...a journey through space—a universal excitement. Our minds are challenged, our imaginations stimulated and we're off on a voyage to other worlds.

Space, however, is a strange thing—it's so invisible. We can't see it, but we *can* see the voyagers traveling in it. *They* are the great immortality of STAR TREK...*they* are our promise of a future.

Each crew member of the *Enterprise* is a "forever personality"—someone we know, someone who maintains standards, someone who can assure us of tomorrow. Indeed, someone we like to think of as a mirror of ourselves.

But something is missing in the reflection. In *Trek or Treat* we're adding it. We're giving earthly follies and frailties to our "forever personalities." We're making faces at our image—we're laughing at ourselves.

Here, then, is STAR TREK—down to earth and strictly off the trek!

...97...98...99...100!
Ready or not, here I come!

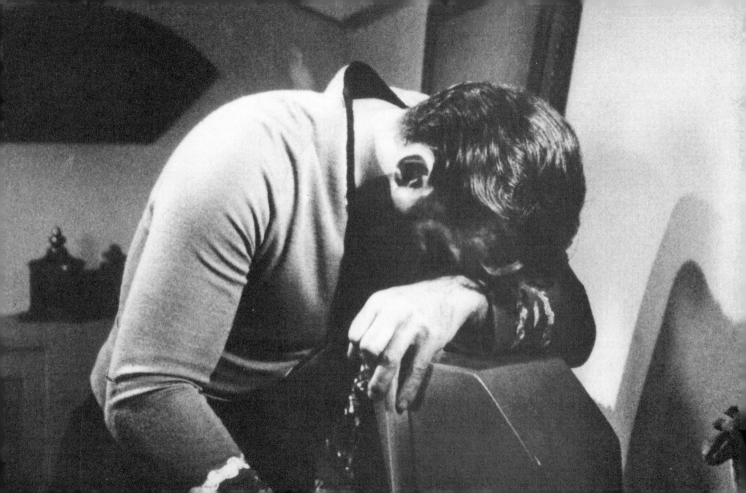

I *said*…no peeking!

You beast! ———————

Would you believe…
I used to be
a 99-pound weakling?

I do *so* have a
sense of humor!

Gee, I didn't know
it was loaded!

Awww...
he faw down and go boom!

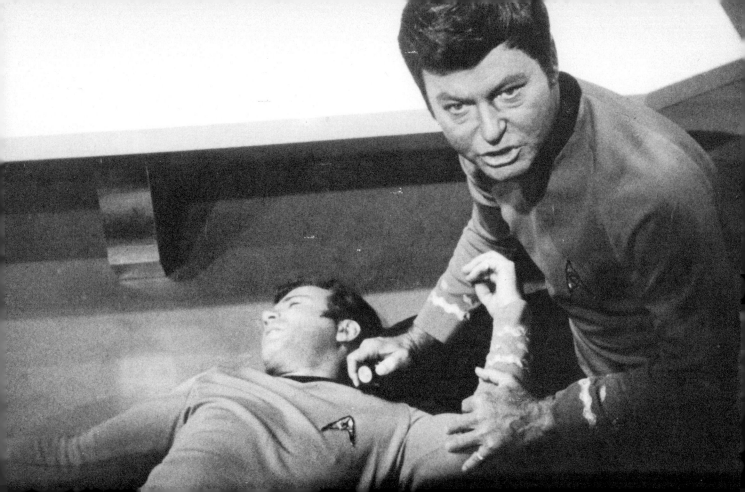

"Kiss it and make it better"?...
Really, Doctor!

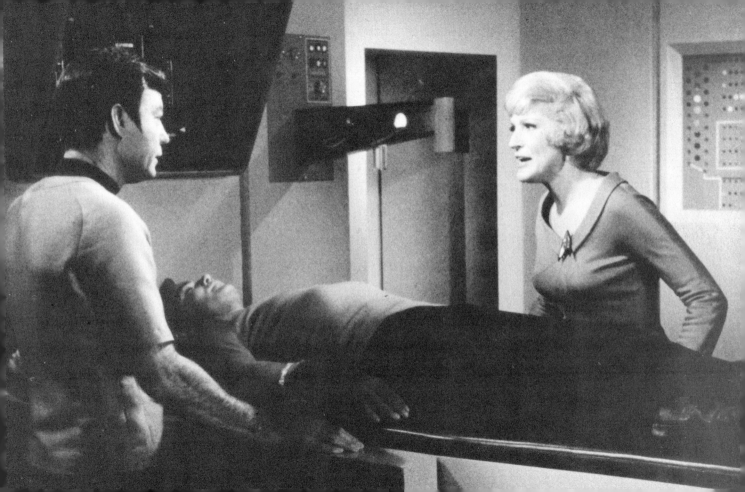

There, there, Captain—
it's only a tetanus shot!

Okay, together now:
"Tea for two and two for tea."

Roy Clark—
eat your heart out!

You're stepping on my foot! ————

Love means never having
to say you're sorry.

Sometimes I think
you only love me for my body. _____

Let's see…
Is it feed a cold and starve a fever
or starve a cold and feed a fever?

We called in a consultant. ———

I have "ring around the collar"?

Don't tell *me* you've been working, Spock… ———
You've been watching the Fonz again!

Will you look at
that long-haired weirdo!

Get a haircut, Son! ———————

Last thing I remember
is telling him to step outside.

It goes well
with your high heels. —————

This is the pits!
Got into my dress blues and now
the party is called off.

Yes, my lovely…
you might say I'm pulling rank!

Anyone for skinny-dipping?

Don't you ever knock?

Okay—who's been writing my number
on the men's room wall?

A little more to the left…
that's good…now scratch.

There will be no more
shuttle service leaving this ship 'til I find out
who took my yo-yo!

Hey, you guys!
It's a complaint to
"Hold it down!"

Second word, first syllable…

Nap time is over, Captain.
Here are your milk and cookies.

I'll have another Shirley Temple.

Why can't they
ever serve sukiyaki?

You're the Welcome Wagon?

The sky's the limit!

Same to you, fella.

Everybody out!
This poolroom is off limits!

Aaaaa-yyy!
'Cause I'm the *Captain!*

I'll thank you to
keep my ears out of this!

Quit bawling!
We'll find you another balloon!

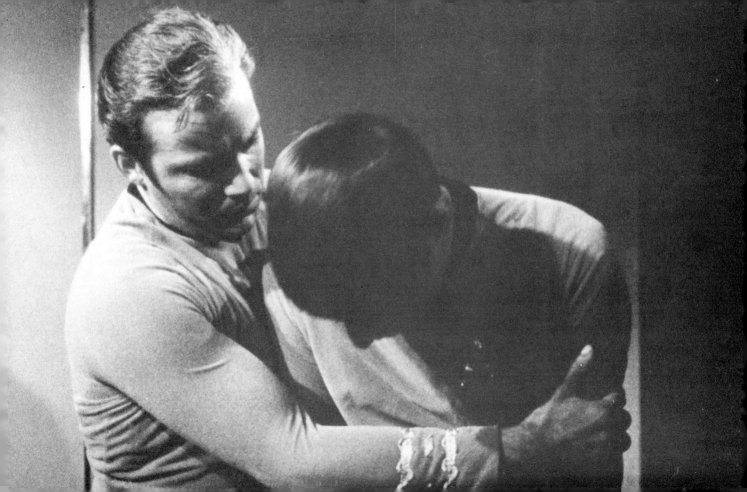

There, there, Spock.
I think you have a *good* sense of humor.
What does everybody else
on this ship know, anyway?

How 'bout it, Rubber Duck,
got your ears on? Get me a 10-81.

I hate these class reunions!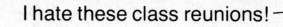

Good night, Captain.

Good night, Dr. McCoy.

Good night, Mr. Spock.

Good night, John Boy.